This
Christmas Cracker
belongs to:

_____

_____

First published 1988 by Walker Books Ltd
87 Vauxhall Walk, London SE11 5HJ
This edition published 2010
2 4 6 8 10 9 7 5 3 1
© 1988 John Rogan
The right of John Rogan to be identified as author/illustrator of this work has been asserted by him
in accordance with the Copyright, Designs and Patents Act 1988
Printed in China
British Library Cataloguing in Publication Data:
a catalogue record for this book is available from the British Library
978-1-4063-3308-4
www.walker.co.uk

The Biggest Snowball Ever!

John Rogan

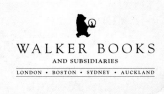

WALKER BOOKS
AND SUBSIDIARIES
LONDON · BOSTON · SYDNEY · AUCKLAND

For Claire

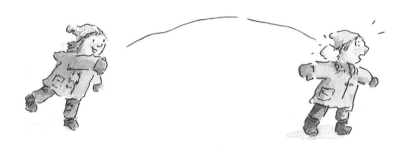

It's Christmas Eve, there's snow outside,
this morning Paul and Claire decide
that after breakfast they will go
to play with friends out in the snow.

They look through drawers and under stairs
to find old clothes that no one wears,

then choose the things that they will take
to dress the snowmen they will make.

The doorbell rings, their friends are here,
all dressed in nice warm winter gear.

And so the children make their way
out to the park this winter's day.

Claire makes her snowman small and fat.

Her brother's wears a big brown hat.

And then Claire grins. She thinks, Tee hee, my brother will be mad with me.

She rolls some snow to make a ball
and chucks it at her brother Paul.

He throws one back but then, oh dear!
It lands in someone else's ear!

And so there is a snowball fight.
The snowballs fly from left and right.

Then Paul gets hit by ten or more
and wants to even up the score.

He walks and walks and walks until
he's reached the summit of the hill

and starts to roll a ball of snow
to aim it at his friends below.

But then he slips, so now poor Paul

becomes part of his own snowball!

The snowball's such a massive size
the children can't believe their eyes!

"It's bigger than my house!" shouts one,
who stumbles when she starts to run.

The snowball gets them one by one
and soon it's like a currant bun

with lots of children stuck in there.
Oh, look! It's caught another pair!

The snowball stops, the children shout,
"Please someone come and help us out!

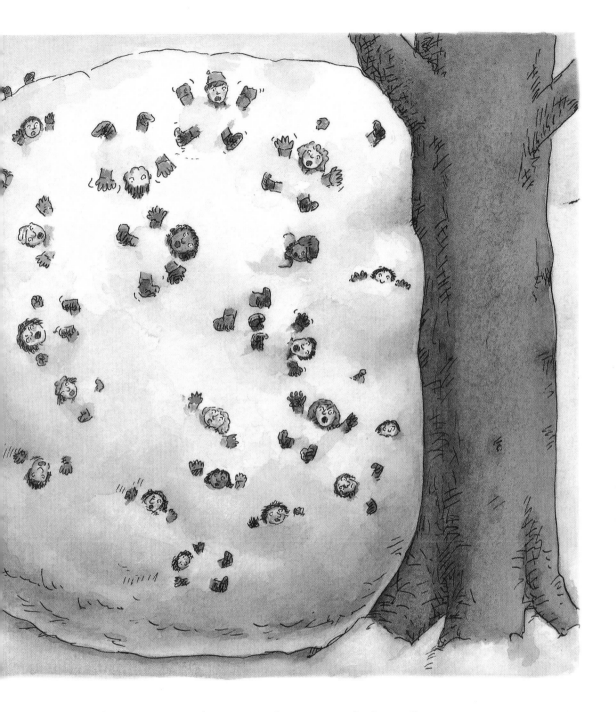

For if we can't get home it's clear
that we'll miss Christmas Day this year!"

Claire runs for help! She shouts like mad,
for things are looking really bad.

Her friends are feeling very glum
inside the snowball frozen numb.

Then neighbours dig with all their might
to save the children from their plight.
The children come out one by one.
The rescue work will soon be done.

Then free at last, and since it's late,
the children do not hesitate.

They wave goodbye, they're on their way because tomorrow's Christmas Day.

At home Paul says, "That must have been the biggest snowball ever seen!"

Before they go to bed, these two
have one more thing they have to do.

Now Paul and Claire are fast asleep
and dream of toys they'd love to keep.

They know that Santa's on his way
to bring them joy on Christmas Day.